SEVEN CAROLS, SEVEN GIFTS

SEVEN CAROLS, SEVEN GIFTS

Christmas Stories For All Ages

by

Drew Bacigalupa

SANTA FE

Sunstone books may be purchased for educational, business,
or sales promotional use. For information please write:
Special Markets Department, Sunstone Press, P.O. Box 2321,
Santa Fe, New Mexico 87504-2321.

Library of Congress Cataloging-in-Publication Data:

Bacigalupa, Drew, 1923–
    Seven carols, seven gifts: Christmas stories for all ages / Drew
Bacigalupa.
        p. cm.
    ISBN: 0-86534-368-3 (pbk.)
    1. Christmas stories, American. I. Title.

PS3552.A25765 S4 2002
813'.54—dc21   2002036485

Published in   SUNSTONE PRESS
            Post Office Box 2321
            Santa Fe, NM 87504-2321 / USA
            (505) 988-4418 / orders only (800) 243-5644
            FAX (505) 988-1025
            www.sunstonepress.com

Madonna of the Fleurs-de-lis

In memory of my mother, Maria Laura Merolla.
She knew more about the human condition than anyone
else I've ever known over a long lifetime.

There is a variety of gifts but always the same Spirit;
there are all sorts of service to be done,
but always to the same Lord;
working in all sorts of ways in different people,
it is the same God who is working in all of them.
The particular way in which the Spirit is given to each
person is for a good purpose.

Corinthians 12:4
Jerusalem Bible

Contents

ILLUSTRATIONS

All illustrations are from original works by the author

Cover: *Madonna,* colored inks

Frontispiece: *Madonna of the Fleurs-de-lis,* casein

Clare and the Magi: *Drawing,* colored inks

A Good and Perfect Gift: *The Pueblo Madonna,* bronze,
approximately 7"h

Broken Boundaries: *Holy Night,* ceramic tile 6" x 12"

Franco and Pirata: *Household Madonna,* bronze
approximately 9"h

Don Lorenzo: *The Holy Family,* ceramic tile 30" x 30"

The Nature of Gifts: *Drawing,* colored inks

El Santo Niño: *La Sagrada Familia,* bronze
approximately 9"h

Epilogue: *Madonna and Child,* pencil drawing

Back cover photo by Ellen Williams Bacigalupa

FOREWORD

If life is to have meaning it must transcend the basics of survival. It is not enough that we compete for sustenance against nature and our own kind, but we need covenants of understanding to place that striving for survival into a kinder, a more humane, order. Drew Bacigalupa draws upon his Catholic background to tell us tales of human interaction, his warm and tender understanding of children, in the framework of that humane order.

I first came to see that universality when, as a Jew in the company of a Palestinian friend, I visited the Church of the Nativity built in Bethlehem by Emperor Constantine. The church overlies the Crypt of the Nativity, the traditional site of the birth of Jesus. It is there one experiences the presence of the manger, the crib that held the earthly body of the immortal child.

Off to the left of the crib and up on the wall hangs a depiction of Jesus, the man. The man is black.

It is this universality that one experiences in reading Drew's heartrending snippets of human lives depicted in all humanity.

—*Joachim Oppenheimer, M. D.*

PREFACE

These seven Christmas stories first appeared separately as newspaper columns and prize-winning short stories in New Mexican competitions over a period of twenty-five years. Two of them were published as slim picture-books, one was adapted to film. Repeated requests for the stories—Christmas carols—initiated publication of this book.

The number seven is symbolic of perfect order, a complete period or cycle, comprising the union of the ternary and the quaternary. It is the number forming the basic series of musical notes, of colors and of the planetary spheres as well as of the gods corresponding to them, the number of the capital sins and their opposing virtues. Of especial interest to me is the symbolism of the Seven Gifts of the Holy Spirit as given in Revelation 5:12—power, riches, wisdom, might, honor, glory and blessing.

—Drew Bacigalupa
Santa Fe, 2002

Acknowledgments

The carols *Clare . . . and the Magi, Don Lorenzo* and *The Nature of Gifts* were first published as columns in Drew Bacigalupa's weekly feature *Coffeebreak Journal* for the Santa Fe *New Mexican* during the 1970s. They were subsequently included in a book-collection of the columns, *Journal of an Itinerant Artist,* published in hardcover by OSV, Inc, Huntington, Indiana, in 1977.

A Good and Perfect Gift (1973), *Franco and Pirata* (1975) and *El Santo Niño* (1993) all appeared first as short stories in Christmas issues of the Santa Fe *New Mexican.*

A Good and Perfect Gift, illustrated by Jeannie Pear, was first published as a picture-book by OSV, Inc, in 1978. The story was later adapted to film, shot on location in Truchas, New Mexico, and released under the same title by Franciscan Communications, Los Angeles, in 1988. Distribution of video cassettes of the film is through *St Anthony Messenger Press, Franciscan Communications,* Cincinnati.

Franco and Pirata, illustrated by Angelo Marelli, was published as a picture-book by Pickwick Publications, Allison Park, PA, in 1985.

Broken Boundaries was first published as the cover story in the weekly Santa Fe *Reporter,* Christmas issue December 19-25, 1990.

CLARE . . . AND THE MAGI

"But now, as I hold Clare's card, its bright image

prompts me to utter the word aloud—Magi."

CLARE ... AND THE MAGI

Our mail is always heavy, but in the few weeks before Christmas it is staggering. Season's greetings come in by the dozens, from all over the world, many from old friends we haven't seen in a quarter century. Cards arrive from mail-order clients we've never met, or tourists who were in our gallery only once; from people we've known briefly at national workshops and conventions, or met on vacations. Forgetful of names, I must ask my wife: Who is this, when was that, do we know him?

The cards are corralled in a huge wooden bowl, and each day they pile higher, eventually spilling over. Some of the signatures on them remain faceless to me, but names have become familiar through yearly repetition. A few are from my army buddies and wartime friends, their names on cards surrounded by those of total strangers—wives and children, grandchildren.

I sometimes think the enormous trough of cards is like a disorganized notebook for an epic Tolstoian novel. Many of the greetings include lengthy notes and long newsletters advising us of births and deaths, marriages and divorces, professional advances or setbacks, relocations and travel. Children we've never met have grown up on those scribbled pages.

We are always too busy before Christmas to peruse the cards at leisure. But in those rare still and quiet moments, perhaps early morning while the rest of the family sleeps, one of us will pause before that towering mound and turn over the cards until one demands attention.

Here is Clare's, as brief and taciturn as ever. I'm aware of the discipline and effort required of him to write anything. So much easier to neglect correspondence and hope our paths will cross again— against the bar at O'Hare probably, between planes in Chicago.

We spent a memorable pre-Christmas week together in '44 at Southampton, though neither of us can lay claim to having seen that great port. We arrived on troop trucks in dark and fog and were herded inside a public park which had been converted into a fenced, guarded, tented debarkation area for France. Blackout and persistent fog prevented us from seeing anything beyond a few yards. We could hear trams and, somewhere outside the perimeters of the park, shoppers, bells, broadcasts of Christmas music. Even daylight hours, locked in fog, gave us no glimpse of anything beyond our tents.

Quartermaster stores were low, we were told, cigarettes and liquor unavailable. A rumor persisted that this was not the case, that supplies were being channeled to the black market. Cries of protest rose against the Supply Sergeant. I remember Clare, a chain-smoker in those days, searching in the rutted, frozen mud for discarded cigarette butts. There was mutinous talk among the men of going over the fence, raiding officers' quarters—anything to get tobacco and a drop of Christmas cheer.

One night we passed the chaplain's tent and heard soldiers inside caroling. The sound was unreal, a sweet sanity no long relevant to anything we now knew. Clare and I walked on. And when, inevitably, the air-raid sirens wailed, we felt a sense of propriety at this return to normalcy. Carols, sentiment, brotherly love— these seemed blasphemous at that time, in that place.

Yet, something more than privation of cigarettes and drink tore at Clare's insides. The dreariness of the camp, the men's surliness, and the sounds of Southampton out beyond the fog kept his nerves raw and his face hard. We silently stomped the ruts together, fighting cold, fighting thoughts of the season. I observed him ministering roughly, with a harsh and angry tenderness, to young green recruits at the breaking point.

Late Christmas Eve, while men huddled morosely about tent stoves, I became aware that Clare had been missing since dusk. And I guessed where. He eventually appeared in the canvas doorway, broad-grinned, his arms piled high with gifts—cartons of cigarettes, boxes of chocolates, and bottles of brandy. The black-market rumors had proven true—and the storehouse vulnerable.

If we thought it then, as merriment spread throughout the camp, we failed to say so. But now, as I hold Clare's card, its bright design prompts me to utter the word aloud—Magi.

A GOOD AND PERFECT GIFT

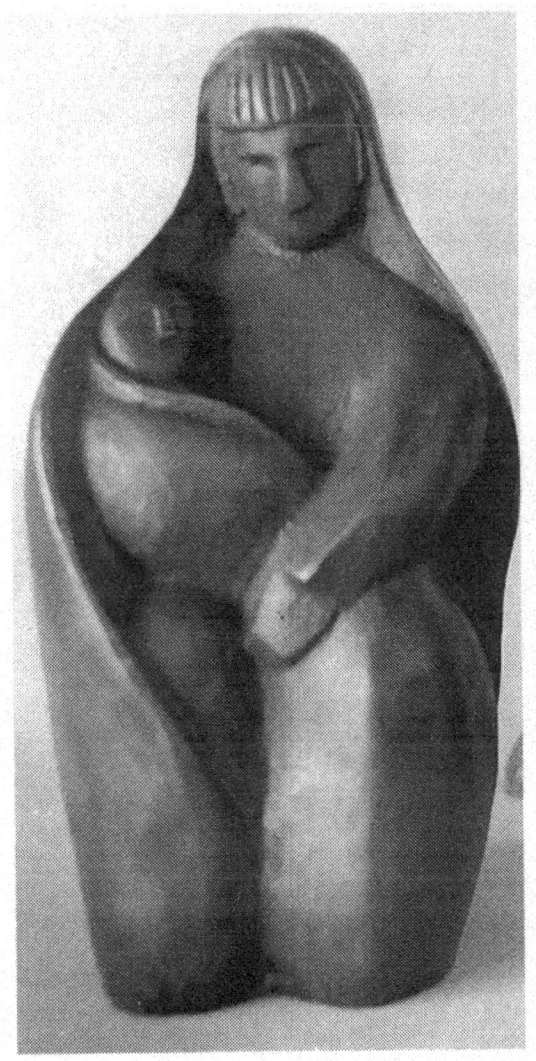

"There'd be only Maria *and* Jesuscristro, *mother and child,*

like Mama and herself, without a San José, *without a father."*

A GOOD AND PERFECT GIFT

She was a little bit mad at *Santo Niño*. It was
Christmas morning and she'd already opened the one
gift under their tree at home. That didn't seem like
much—a winter sweater which she needed anyway, no
toy, and no sign of the Daddy she'd asked for. She
could excuse Santa Claus, maybe he just forgot, but
El Santo Niño wasn't supposed to forget anything.

And it seemed she'd been asking for him as long
as she could remember—not for something impossible,
like Mama said, not for a Daddy she could have all the
time like the other kids, just for a Daddy for one day,
for Christmas day.

It was cold in church and the Mass was long,
and Mama kept her head bowed, crying. If she fidgeted,
Mama reproved her sharply, "Manuelita!" and made her
look again at the *Nacimiento.*

But Manuelita wasn't happy about that Baby. He had both father and mother, and lots of *pastores* keeping them company, and sheep and a cow and a *burro,* and shiny lighted stars above His stable, and a tree behind that was bigger and prettier than hers.

And when she looked away, she saw other little girls in church standing next to daddies, or being held by them, and carrying in their arms the most beautiful dolls in the whole wide world.

After Mass, she and Mama trudged through deep snow up the hill to their *adobe* at the edge of the village. *Piñon* smoke was coming from every chimney but theirs. Mama held her hand tightly, but they were silent. Manuelita didn't want silence on Christmas and wondered if the radio batteries were still working. Mama had kept it on a long time last night. She was thinking of that and of how maybe she could hear some carols or stories when Mama pushed open their door— and gasped in fright!

Peering around Mama's frayed *rebozo,* Manuelita saw a man standing at their kitchen table, facing them with a gun in his hand. *Santo Niño* had remembered. It was her Christmas Daddy.

He was very tall, almost as high as the roof *vigas,* and had a big black mustache and heavy, dark eyebrows. He carried a bag, too—not stuffed with toys like Santa Claus' but with other things, maybe presents. Manuelita could see a blanket roll, a hatchet, some tins of food and the bloodied pelt of a rabbit he'd probably recently killed with that gun.

He and Mama were talking fast, saying funny things like "It's on the radio; I know who you are," and "If you let me stay a little while, I won't hurt anyone." Mama thought he was a bad man, and didn't like him; and Manuelita, wanting to explain who he really was, kept trying to get her attention by pulling at her arm. After a while they stopped talking and stared at each other. Then Mama just sat in a chair, like she was very tired and couldn't move.

Manuelita went to her side and whispered in her ear that he was her Christmas present, the Daddy she'd asked *Santo Niño* to give her for just this one day. Mama cried again, but she didn't speak. Then she wiped her eyes with the back of her hand and crossed the room to a pot of *frijoles* she'd been preparing before Mass.

The man hitched the gun in his belt and pulled the rabbit from the bag and spilled out all the canned foods on the kitchen table.

Mama wouldn't let her go with him, but Manuelita watched from the frosted window when he ran to the woods behind their house and came back with armloads of *piñon*. He set the logs ablaze in their corner fireplace and stood with his back to it, keeping warm.

Manuelita went and stood beside him, putting her hands behind her as he did, spreading her feet in the widest possible stance.

Mama glanced at her and started to speak, but then was silent and turned again to preparing the meal. For the first time, though she'd never stopped looking at him, the man's eyes rested on Manuelita.

"We have a little Christmas tree, but no *Nacimiento,*" she said. "That's not right, is it?"

"No, *mi hija,*" the man answered, "but perhaps we can do something about that."

Maybe her Daddy was a *santero,* the kind Mama had told her about, who carved saints from the soft cottonwood and took them off the mountain down into the city where *gringos* and places called museums paid good money for them. He must be one because nobody else could put a knife to plain old wood and so soon have it looking like real people, better than the *santos* in the village church!

She watched his big hands shaping the delicate contours of the Baby, marveling that *Santo Niño* had sent her a Daddy better than all the others in the village, where they had no *santero*. And when she picked up the shavings, the man took her frail hands into his rough callused ones and showed her how to fashion simple ornaments from scraps of wood tied together with thread. All afternoon they huddled by the fireplace, busy at work.

Manuelita made enough ornaments to decorate the small tree from top to bottom all around, and when they stirred, the raw wood picked up glints of firelight, like little stars dancing among the green boughs. The man completed a *Niño,* a beautiful Babe on a bed of straw, and began to carve *Nuestra Señora.* He smoked a big brown pipe as he worked, and let the child hold flaming kindling to light it each time he packed it with fresh tobacco.

At one moment during the darkening day, Manuelita heard a rare and lovely sound in the room. When she looked up, it was Mama singing softly to herself as she patted out *tortillas* at the kitchen table.

They had a grand *comida*; the rabbit was very good, tender, with lots of it in every *taco.* Mama had added some of Daddy's dried *chili* to the *frijoles*, and Manuelita savored the pungent flavor in her mouth. No one spoke much, which did not seem unusual to Manuelita, but occasionally the man made a silly joke and they all laughed.

Manuelita knew that this was the best meal of her life, and the best day she'd ever lived. One tiny disappointment clouded her joy, but she could not bring herself to speak of it. Night was coming, Christmas was ending, and there wouldn't be time for Daddy to finish the *Nacimiento*. There'd be only *Maria* and *Jesuscristo*, mother and child like Mama and herself, without a *San José*, without a father.

She wanted to stay awake through the last minute of the evening, but fatigue claimed her and she lay down sleepily before the fire. Mama covered her with an old *poncho*. Manuelita watched her mother and the man sit opposite each other at the table, not speaking but listening to carols on the radio. Sometimes, when there were news broadcasts, they turned up the volume and exchanged solemn glances. Manuelita fell asleep with the vision of firelight radiantly bathing Mama and her beautiful strong Daddy.

The fire was almost out when she woke, the room only dimly lighted, and the man was gone. She was on her cot; he must have carried her there, for scraps of his pipe tobacco were on her blanket. She scooped them up as treasures. Mama slept soundly on her narrow bed across the room.

Manuelita felt no sorrow that the man was gone, only joy that she'd had a Daddy on Christmas Day. She got up and tiptoed across the room to see again the *Nacimiento* and thank *El Santo Niño* for answering her prayers.

And there with *Nuestra Señora* and the Infant was a third carving, unfinished, only roughly blocked out, with no facial features and no details. But it was unmistakably *San José*, the father of the family, standing tall beside *Maria*, his head bowed toward *El Niño*. Mama had lighted a vigil candle before them, and for a long time Manuelita sat and stared at the beautiful figures.

Broken Boundaries

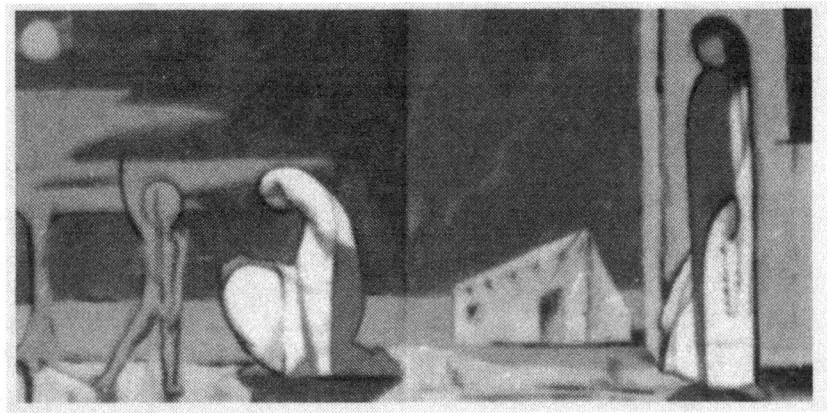

"Tonight, this noche de paz, *this birthday of your* Santo Niño,

you dump these needy strangers, needy children, in my lap."

Broken Boundaries

Luis, in the moment of awakening, couldn't remember whether they'd crossed the border or not, whether he was traveling in the States or was still in Mexico. He'd been so tired and dozed so much of this trip.

Being old could be a nuisance. Wasn't at all like when he was younger and remained wide awake for hours, even through the nights, reluctant to surrender watching the towns, and, particularly, *la tierra.*

But, of course, this was the States. He now drowsily recalled changing buses at Juarez-El Paso, automatically going through the familiar ritual of customs. He must have drifted immediately into sleep again, for the huge crowded vehicle had traveled less than 50 miles from the border, was lumbering through Doña Ana Valley. He'd worked the fields here many years ago, had worked so many fields between Torreon and Santa Fe. The land didn't really change. People did, and what they erected upon the land did. But the Rio, with its twisted ribbon of trees and shrubs, irrigated farms as it always had; the Organ Mountains soared majestically in the east, and to the west lay the low profile of Picacho Peak. I know it like the back of my hand, Luis thought, all of the land north and south of the border—and that boundary line no longer holds meaning for me. It is one vast *tierra encantada*, glorious country, and mine. I recognize no frontier.

Some of the passengers began to sing. *Feliz Navidad*. They were a mixed cargo, Mexicans and Spanish-Americans, with quite a few blond gringos, college kids, among them. Going home, or to visit relatives, for the holidays. They sang lustily, as if their loud voices could successfully dispel the discomfort and loneliness of sitting among strangers on a rattling bus on Christmas Eve.

Luis' seat companion was, fortunately, a boy in his early teens. Someone who'd take no interest in an old man and not attempt to provoke conversation. The boy's mother and two younger sisters shared a seat farther back in the bus. They were from Old Mexico, *campesinos*; and the youngster, perhaps frightened or intimidated by his first trip away from home, was exceptionally quiet. For that, Luis was grateful. He'd had enough of kids—his own, and his children's children, too. The past year without them in Torreon had been a needed respite from all their demands.

Still, he was going back. His daughter Maida had written that they all missed him, wanted him home among them, not just for *Navidad* but permanently. Certainly his huge ranch north of Santa Fe, with its numerous adobe *casitas* spread over the vast acreage, held room enough for all of them. His favorite house, in the west quarter, had been left untenanted, awaiting his return. None of the family understood, Maida wrote, why he persisted on long visits to Mexico after he'd spent most of his life as a United States citizen, prospered in the States and raised his family there. He belonged, she argued, with his own children and grandchildren.

I belong in no one place, Luis thought. But Maida couldn't know that. She'd never understand, born in the States and ignorant of poverty, how the old ways and values still influenced so much of his behavior. "Papa," she scolded during the expensive phone call to him last week, "you're not poor but rich now, and can afford to take a plane. Why do you insist on dirty old buses?" She didn't know yet, after all these years, that he preferred the bus, preferred to travel slowly between his two homelands, to see again at close range the mesas and mountains, the dry arroyos and flowing ritos, the chamisa, yucca and cacti. And yes, the people, no matter that he long ago had despaired of community and elected to go his own way alone.

The college youths persisted in repetitious choruses of their song. *Feliz Navidad, I Wanna Wish You A Merry Christmas.* Some of them walking in the aisle, visiting friends scattered throughout the bus, passing bottles of wine and tins of beer. The driver, acknowledging the Christmas spirit, made no objection; in fact, seemed to enjoy the diversion. Luis and the boy beside him did not sing. The *muchacho* seemed as indifferent as the old man to the festiveness swelling about them.

They think Christmas makes a difference, Luis pondered. It does not. One day a year of reaching out, seeking brotherhood, and then it's right back to life's jungle, dog-eat-dog. He was traveling toward what Maida called a family reunion, but held no illusions that his sons and daughters had abandoned old feuds among them. Blood was blood, and it was right that he see them again. But with Maria gone, it was not the same. Even now, the empty ache that drove him to Torreon a year ago cramped his chest.

For many years now, he'd held no more faith in the family than in anything else. When you were as old as he was, you knew that everything and everyone ultimately disappointed you —women, children, government, the church, society, fiestas; Christmas, too.

Sons left home to pursue their own interests. Daughters married men who, perhaps simply because they were men, brought new problems into the family. Infants sickened and died—and even a beautiful, perfect baby girl could be snatched from you. And the memory stay with you for more than half a century. You ended up alone; and no person, no thing and no event changed that.

And yet, deep down, there was always that small nagging of hope—like an unborn child —saying this time, perhaps, it will be different.

He closed his eyes against the noise and distraction. It was always better now to shut things out. He was practiced at it, an expert, and within seconds had escaped once more into sleep.

They were well up the Rio when he wakened again. On the east lay the Jornada del Muerto, that awesome desert through which his ancestors, the Conquistadores, had first traveled by foot and horseback. Like him, they had seen the land as one vast country, from Tenochtitlan to Colorado, and acknowledged no boundaries but those fashioned by *El Buen Pastor*. And these—mountains, rivers and deserts—they overcame, as he had, too, in the push northward. It pleased him to think that he may have succeeded where his forefathers failed. Their Cibola proved to be made of adobe dust, not gold; his rancho and haciendas were real, proud monuments to his triumph over generations of poverty. He hadn't been any older than the boy beside him when he'd taken the first journey north toward his own cities of gold.

The *muchacho* was no longer alone, Luis realized. His smaller sister had joined him from the back of the bus. No older than seven, considerably more active than her brother, she sat upon the boy's lap but continuously brushed against the old man. Luis' disapproving frown merely produced a wide grin on her pretty brown face.

"Be still," the boy cautioned the girl in Spanish.

"But I can't see past *el viejo* out the window," the child answered in a dialect which Luis recognized as Zacatecan. She leaned across him, her long black hair under his stubbled chin.

"We can exchange places," Luis, though reluctant to relinquish his window seat, suggested to the boy.

"*No, gracias, señor*," the boy replied. "She'll only want to go back and forth to my mother and sister, anyway. It's best to stay on the aisle."

"Can I sit on *your* lap, then?" the girl asked Luis.

"No," her brother answered. "And don't disturb

the gentleman again, or I'll take you back to Mamacita."

The bus was now quiet. Looking about, Luis saw that many of the passengers, including the rough college crowd, were napping. He caught the eye of the mother of the children beside him, her older daughter sprawled half on the seat and half across the woman's body. The mother, thin and wiry, looked extremely tired and perhaps frightened. She acknowledged Luis' look with a slight bow of her head.

The girl had pressed a tiny elbow hard against Luis' groin. She couldn't seem to sit still.

"There's nothing to see, *niña*," the old man scolded her. "It's not much different from your own country or all the desert we've crossed today."

"But where is Albuquerque?" the child demanded of her brother. "You said it would be a big *norteamericano* city, with tall buildings and lighted Christmas trees and rich gringos everywhere. Like in the pictures you showed me."

"We're still a few hours away from that," Luis grumbled, pushing her toward her brother.

"I'll take her back to Mama," the boy suggested. "Come on, Juanita."

"No, Pancho! I'll be quiet, and not move."

For the first time, Luis noticed that the girl's

legs were bound in steel braces, and observed that the children's poverty was like a brand, indelibly stamped, as his own had been so many years ago.

Pancho turned away from the old man and sat silently staring straight ahead. Luis recognized that defense against worlds other than one's own. "I didn't know your sister was lame," he muttered. "She can sit at the window."

"She must learn that she can't have everything she wants just because of the bad legs. Papa used to spoil her because of that."

The boy spoke matter-of-factly, without emotion. Staring at his dispassionate image, Luis felt strangely as if he were looking into a mirror, at himself as a youth. The toughness essential to survival. Juanita's big eyes, mischievous and unrepentant, held his.

"Papa didn't spoil me," she whispered. "He was just good to me. We're going to visit his grave, *señor*."

"Be quiet, Juanita," he brother commanded.

"No, no, let her speak." Luis, acutely mindful of the girl's lameness, felt she should be denied nothing.

"She doesn't always know what she's talking about," Pancho said.

"Are you really on a pilgrimage?" Luis asked. "To your father's grave?"

"Partly. He's buried on the rancho where he was

working near Taos. Killed last summer in a truck accident. And Mama wants to take Juanita to *el santuario* at Chimayo to rub the holy mud on her legs. They believe in miracles."

It sounded so much like himself. "And you don't believe in miracles," Luis said.

"I believe I must find work up here, as Papa did."

"That is difficult even for grown men. What makes you think yourself, a mere boy, can manage that?"

"He thinks he already is a grown man," Juanita taunted.

"I'm the man of *this* family now," Pancho forcibly told her, "and you, and Consuelo, and Mama, too, will do as I say. We'll live in the north, and we will be rich and we will have doctors to take care of your legs, as Papa wanted."

Juanita heaved an impatient sigh and rolled her eyes at Luis. He felt her small fingers land lightly on his creased, callused hand. When he attempted to draw away, the child's grasp tightened. He offered no further resistance.

Light was beginning to fade, the eastern mountains taking on that crimson glow that always seemed most spectacular at this season of the winter solstice. Father north, they called that stain on the sierras *El Sangre de Cristo*—blood of Christ.

As the bus approached the town of Belen, passengers stirred to view the smoking chimneys, lighted trees in windows and yards, the modest but festive civic decorations of this village on the Rio Grande named for Bethlehem. *Vamos Todos a Belen.* Even as he remembered the old hymn, Luis heard someone in the bus softly humming its melody.

Juanita, drowsing, her head against the old man's shoulder, was missing the lights. Her brother, though awake, appeared to take no interest in the passing landscape. Luis was annoyed that he could not successfully ignore the children. They were so young, so vulnerable, and were getting to him. Pancho's infinitely sad face was too much a reproach of the disillusion and cynicism which had taken root in himself when he was the boy's age, and had crucially dominated his senior years. No child should be so badly scarred. And the girl's frail legs, rigidly encased in steel, would never support her slender body, never permit her to walk straight and bold, upright. Holy mud, doctors, nor anything else were likely to change that.

God, Luis pleaded, why did you put them next to me? I'm old, *Señor*, and have had decades of my own troubles, my own people. Family and friends have drained, exhausted me for as long as I can remember. I'm tired and want relief from human mischief in my final years. *Señor*, you know that; but, *Señor*, you always play me dirty tricks. Tonight, this *noche de paz*, this birthday of your *Santo Niño*, you dump these strangers, needy children, in my lap. And all I've ever wanted, ever asked of you, *Señor,* is to free me from a lifetime of bondage and service to others. Let me rest. I've earned it!

He clutched again at sleep, but this time it eluded him. Behind closed eyes, for long minutes, he resolutely refused to gaze on the world.

Juanita was tugging at his coat. He felt the child skillfully ease her twisted body from her napping brother's arms onto his weary thighs. Through half-raised eyelids, he observed her successful occupation of new territory, her victorious possession of the window. She pressed her nose against the glass, and Luis heard her whispered cries of delight at first sight of the lights of Albuquerque.

Snow was falling, lightly and gently, not heavily enough to quench the *farolitos* already lighting paths to the city's homes. The flickering candles within brown paper-bags stretched for miles, outlining rooftops and terraces of the adobe house, illuminating walkways, circling gardens and climbing staircases. Luis surrendered his pretense of sleep to mutter an explanation to Juanita.

"The *farolitos* are to light the way of *El Santo Niño* into the people's houses."

"Of course," the child answered, impatiently. "What else would they be for!"

She had a quick tongue. Well, he was accustomed to that among the females in his family. And he had well known, but not experienced for a while, the sweetness of a child upon his knees, her head against his chest. But sentiment was a trap, and he didn't want to be trapped. Not again, not still again in these, the quiet years of his life.

The passengers were exceedingly silent, a few asleep, but most gazing out at the lights of the holy night, mindful of their journey's end and imminent reunion with loved ones. Then Juanita began to sing, tenderly, a familiar refrain—*Jesus Es Mi Amor*—and other voices joined her. She touched Luis' lips, inviting him to accompany them, but he'd forgotten how to praise. And, startled, he realized that the child's fingers had touched upon his cheek a tear from ducts he'd long believed gone dry.

Pancho, wakened, put a hand upon his sister's arm. "Come back to me, *niña*. You're disturbing the *señor.*"

"Let her be," Luis said.

"This is Albuquerque?" the boy asked.

"End of the line," Luis responded. "I change

buses for Santa Fe. Where are you headed?"

"Nowhere tonight. We'll go north in the morning."

"Where will you sleep?"

"In the depot."

The bus, its terminal merely blocks away, was winding through the narrow downtown streets. Passengers began gathering their hand luggage. Juanita kept her nose pressed against the window, her eyes wide at the commercial decorations. Luis' legs ached under her light weight, but he did not attempt to move her.

Ah, *Señor*, he thought, you've hooked me again.

And to the boy he said, suddenly, reluctantly, "Would you work for me? I have a ranch north of Santa Fe."

Pancho's reply was unhesitant. "I will work for anyone who pays a fair wage—enough to support my mother and sisters."

'My own children and grandchildren live in houses on the ranch. But one *casita* is mine. Your family could share it with me."

"Mama is a good worker, and so am I. Consuelo is already accustomed to chores. Juanita, of course, cannot work."

Of course, Luis thought. And she'll need looking after, and who else but I will do it when your mother's busy. And doctors should see her legs, and who will pay for that. And Pancho and the older sister should be in school, not at labor, and how could one deny them education. There'd be problems with visas and immigration papers, but he knew all the politicos at the state house—they, governor included, owed him favors, so who better could sponsor and fight for these *probrecitos.*

"Go ask your mother if she's agreeable."

"I will tell her. She leaves decisions to me."

"Tell her, too, that I make no promises, no guarantees, that it's a trial arrangement. I don't want you thinking I can solve all your problems."

"We know that, *señor.*"

"I don't believe in miracles."

"Nor do I, *señor.*"

The boy very gravely, formally, shook Luis' hand. Then he went to the rear of the bus to speak with his mother. Juanita, who'd appeared disinterested in the pragmatic conversation, suddenly turned from the window and kissed Luis. "Silly *abuelo,*" she whispered, "and silly Pancho. Of course there are miracles."

She was a flirt. Well, he'd always been susceptible to that.

The bus was turning into the depot. Luis knew what he'd have to do. First things first. Phone Maida to begin with, and say he'd not be in until tomorrow.

She'd be furious, of course, but then she was used to his infuriating her. Get this little family to a good dinner, and then a motel, and somehow make travel arrangements for the morning. Could he rent a car so late over the holiday? Well, there were commuter planes, always the buses, one could even likely hire a taxi for an exorbitant holiday fee. You have money now, spend it, Maida was constantly advising him.

Jaunita rocked back and forth across his knees, anxious to be off the bus, for the adventure to begin. "That hurts my old bones," he said, and lightly cuffed her. The child grinned. Pancho was making his way forward with his weary mother, Consuelo, and their ragged assortment of parcels.

For one second before they joined him, Luis closed his eyes and took a deep breath. Ah, *Buen Señor,* you've won again—given me still another burden! Now, in my old age! But no doubt You think You know what's best. So it's people again.

He let Pancho take Juanita from him and watched the boy expertly carry her from the bus. He followed the children's mother onto the loading platform. In the terminal, the public address system was raucously blaring the carols of *Navidad*.

Franco and pirata

"Mama and his teachers were angry with him

because he continued to mope over a lost dog."

Franco and Pirata

Franco stared at the Tiber. The waters were calm now, silvery grey with just the first tint of gold touching playful currents circling Isola Tiberina. How he hated this once beloved river; and dreaded the errands which Mama kept sending him on—errands which constantly required him to cross one of the bridges. This time she wanted a special herb to spice the Christmas dinner, and though Franco had argued that the seasoning could be purchased closer to home, Mama insisted that he take the long walk into Trastevere and her favorite shop.

Christmas dinner! What kind of a Christmas would it be without Pirata? He had done everything he could think of to get the dog back—governed his behavior at home and at school, lighted candles to the Madonna at Santa Sabina, checked the dog pounds, even scribbled a note to the Santo Bambino and carried it himself across town to lay at the Infant's feet in the shrine at Santa Maria Aracoeli. Nothing had worked. Mama and all his teachers were angry with him because he continued to mope over a lost dog. "It was only an animal, and now it's undoubtedly dead," they all insisted. "You should be ashamed to go about each day with such a long face." But they didn't know Pirata like he did. How could you say "it's only an animal" about something as special as Pirata?

He remembered his older brother Tonino handing the puppy to him last Christmas day, a long year ago, explaining that he was short of lire but had purchased this mutt at the Flea Market for a few coins. "You said a dog was what you wanted more than anything in the whole world, Franco," Tonino whispered, holding the small boy by the shoulders and looking gravely into his eyes. "For once in this family, somebody should have what they most want. She ain't much to look at—just a cowering pup—but I give her to you and she's all yours."

There was an explosion, of course. Mama threw up her arms, invoked all the saints, mercilessly berated Tonino. He was a ne'er-do-well who quit jobs because they bored him, who lived in the coffee bars and cinemas, stayed out all night with disreputable companions, and was now bringing a half-starved ugly dog into her home.

Crossing herself and kissing her fingertips,

Mama recited a long and passionate litany on the evils of canines. They had fleas, were mangy, never housebroken and went rabid. They ate much more they were entitled to, and polluted the streets of Rome. Females swelled up and bore litters—twice a year!—and how was she supposed to dispose of those creatures. God continued to rain punishment on her through a wayward older son who was now out to corrupt her sainted little boy and subvert his promise of scholarship and a decent life among the educated.

"Through the holidays only," she finally conceded, "and then, Franco, you find some other imbecile to take this latest cross from me."

Pirata was certainly ungainly, a skinny little thing with a large wobbly skull and enormous paws. She was of indistinct coloring as well as lineage, neither black, tan or gray but a haphazard blending of all three. One pointed ear remained erect while the other drooped. Franco was under orders to restrict the pup to Mama's wall-bound laundry terrace, but Pirata whimpered so pitifully the first night that he rescued her and stealthily brought her to his bed. She slept on his chest against his heart beat. The next morning, and from then on, they were inseparable.

Except, of course, while he was at school. For when the holidays ended, the boy and Mama entered into a daily pact whereby he was to keep the dog "one more day" depending on his scholastic grades and strict execution of all assigned chores. Not that Mama liked Pirata—named by Tonino for a vaguely delineated eye-patch and her pirating of any unattended food—even though the dog made frequent friendly overtures to the busy, bustling, harassed mistress of the home.

Franco quickly housebroke his pet, but Mama did not relent of her rule that the dog remain cloistered within the laundry terrace. Pirata came into the apartment only when Franco smuggled her into his room. He was rather amazed that Mama, otherwise so vigilant, didn't hear him do that night after night.

Pirata grew so fast, Franco worried that she'd never stop. Mama observed her growth with a baleful eye, lamenting to the good Gesu that her prodigal sons had foisted a mutant pony on their poor widowed mother. And in the nights Franco would whisper and plead with Pirata to please stop, not grow any more. They day finally came when the skull and the paws seemed to fit her body, and Tonino assured Franco that the dog was "just about there." Mama was by now in great alarm that soon she'd be having grand-puppies, but Tonino fixed that, too. He had a friend on the Veneto who was a veterinarian and who lusted to meet one of the signorinas from the film studios at Cinecitta. Tonino knew everybody, inside and outside Rome, and traded the spaying of Pirata for an introduction to a really important neighborhood celebrity, a big bleached blonde who'd had not one but two walk-on parts in Fellini movies.

Franco was wise to city traffic, and no dog of his was going to take its chances against Roman drivers. He turned over to Mama every lira earned from his Saturday job with Zio Giacomo, so there was no money for a collar and leash. But Franco fashioned these from good stout rope and took pride in walking Pirata through the nearby fashionable streets of the Aventine. Every day he encountered fastidious *signori* with their groomed and pedicured thoroughbreds— poodles and shepherds, for the most part—but he wouldn't have traded Pirata for any of them. She was better behaved than all other dogs in the district, obeying his commands, not straining at the leash, barking or seeking mischief with nosey canines or an occasional stray cat. Pirata, with her great size and strength, could have broken loose from Franco any time she cared to. But she stayed close to his side, in cadence with his short steps, ignoring seductive sights and smells on all sides. A proud moment for Franco came one afternoon in Piazza Bocca della Verita when he overheard an elegant signora chiding her muzzled setter for his unmanageable behavior. "Why can't you be a good doggy like that little boy's is."

She had to run, and the best place to turn her

loose was on the immense field of the Circus Maximus. Even when older boys gathered there to practice *calcio*, the huge arena easily accommodated the sprinting Pirata and a knot of soccer players. Professore Bugnini had been lecturing on the Roman Empire at school for months; now Franco shared some of the old man's excitement for his subject. Watching Pirata charge around the corso, the boy could conjure visions of horses and chariots; and sometimes the ball players would pause at their game to cheer on the splendid animal, and Franco heard the roar of Caesar's crowds. Towering above and beyond them, the ruins of the Palatine, though flushed with crimson under a setting sun, blazed for Franco with glistening marbles of the original imperial palaces.

He had a dog of courage. He could command her to jump from the highest heights or leap the widest chasms, and she obeyed without hesitation. She was an excellent retriever, fetching anything he threw. Once on an excursion to Ostia in a car Tonino had borrowed, Franco and his brother spent the best part of a morning casting objects far into the pounding surf and marveling at Pirata's fearless recovery of them. She had learned to carry objects in her mouth—Franco's books, shopping parcels, even to take the mail from the postman without leaving a drop of saliva or tooth mark on the packet.

On Saturdays, Pirata accompanied Franco to

Campo dei Fiori where they assisted Zio Giacomo at his butcher stall in the open market. They boy's uncle was a stern boss, which Pirata instantly recognized. She disciplined her piratical instincts about meat, taking her post at the side of the stall and never moving except on command. Franco helped at waiting on customers, running errands, and was responsible for persistent cleanup of the small area. Zio didn't approve of the dog in the beginning but later came to realize that Pirata helped his trade. Customers who had deserted him for other butchers now returned to Zio Giacomo because they wanted to pet or admire Pirata, whom they likened to the she-wolf — *"la lupa"* — and her role in the origins of Rome. Many customers insisted that Zio or Franco give their packaged meat orders to Pirata to bring to them—and nodded heads in appreciation as the large animal, superbly self-disciplined, gently placed the tantalizingly aromatic packages in their hands. *"Che phenomena!"* they'd exclaim, and always comment on the close camaraderie between boy and dog. The team enjoyed a kind of fame in Campo dei Fiori—a familiar and pleasant diversion for a population which still sought most of its entertainment in the piazzas. At day's end, Zio Giacomo rewarded Franco with very little lire but always a basket of meat-cuts to take home to Mama. And always some choice bones and morsels for Pirata.

It was a good time. But one day after summer's

end, Franco returned from school to an unusual sight. Mama was seated at the kitchen table, apparently oblivious to the mound of take-in mending before her, and Pirata was not exiled to the laundry terrace but sat with her head in Mama's lap. Mama was crying, not loudly as she often did, but very softly, and Pirata joined her with mournful whimpering. Mama waved Franco aside; and when he went to his room, Pirata most unexpectedly did not follow but remained with her head under the woman's hand. Toward evening, Franco learned that Zia Benedicta—Mama's favorite younger sister—had died at her home in Orvieto. Mama was gone for a few days. When she returned from the funeral, she brought with her a new and shining collar and leash for Pirata. The dog grew very attached to these possessions and if for any reason Franco removed her collar, carried it to him in her mouth and whined until he put it back on.

Professore Bugnini was assigning selected students to compose verses and speeches which they were to deliver, in the traditional way, from the pulpit at Santa Maria Aracoeli. These were addressed to the Santo Bambino, who was moved from His chapel to the *presepio*, or creche, for the Christmas holidays. Franco, guiltily, had begun to neglect school work. He was tired of the constant effort to maintain top grades. Some of the boys not chosen to compose verses taunted him about being the professore's favorite and said that the annual ceremony with the Bambino was a farce—all those Mamas' boys were blownup little Ciceros, dressed to the nines, spouting off nonsense to a bejeweled babydoll. Tonino, too, had been advising him to grow up, escape the softness of Mama and teachers. "Rome is a jungle," his older brother counseled, "and you've got to learn to survive in it. You're too good, Franco, and the cannibals in the streets eat up the good guys. Grow some claws."

Franco wasn't growing any claws but he was considering Tonino's words. Certainly, much of what he saw about him in the piazzas didn't correspond with what Mama, his teachers and the priests had to say about the goodness of man. And he was discovering that to be more popular with classmates he had to be less studious, less exemplary, and spend more time in the streets. The verse for the Bambino didn't get written. Grades on papers tumbled. Mama wasn't quite herself since Zia's death—Franco could count on her not to get after him for a while.

When the November rains came, the boys rushed from school to watch the wild river and to race down *lungotevere* kicking up massed leaves and shattered tree branches. There were floods north of the city, many Tiber bridges were closed, and *Il Messagero* headlined that the city was paralyzed. For four days the torrents and winds persisted, the Romani abandoning businesses, sulking, venturing out only when necessary. But Franco plunged deliriously into the holocaust with his new chums, Pirata on her shiny leash racing at his side or skittering freely through the swampy corso of the Circus. His friends took the boy far afield, to the Janiculum and up to Piazza di Spagna, over to the neon arcades near Stazione Termini where Mama had expressly forbade him ever to go. He watched the youths lounging at espresso bars, saw the pickpockets plying their trade among the tourists, and understood— in amazement—that some of the boys moving knowingly among the sodden crowds were not much older than himself. The Termini was mysterious, exhilarating and dangerous in a way his own neighborhood could never be.

On the last day of the rains while the swollen river tumbled with debris and uprooted trees, Franco and his friends jaunted to Isola Tiberina for close inspection of the raging waters. The explored the perimeter of the small island, delighting in its conformity to the shape of a ship, pretending they were sailors of old tossing whatever trash they could find over the side and watching it quickly disappear in the currents. Pirata had been as rebellious as Franco in recent weeks, and now she broke loose from him, racing at the water's edge, barking wildly at the taunts of his friends. A religious medical brother from the island's pharmacy, his black robe swirling about him in the fierce wind, scolded them and ordered them to return to their homes. But as they were about to obey him, one of the boys caught Pirata and ripped the collar with leash from her throat. With a huge, grand, expansive wave of his arm he tossed it high in the air and into the Tiber. The dog immediately went after it.

With pounding heart, Franco watched Pirata swept downstream. Within seconds, she could no longer be seen.

Now the island was like a postcard, serene between the bridges linking it to east and west banks, turning more golden by the moment under the setting sun. Soon the festive city lights would be raised, bells would toll from the hill, and the people prepare for midnight Mass. Mama would take him to church, and Franco was sure to be uncomfortable. For he was angry with the Bambino and—Christmas Eve or not— couldn't manage to forgive Him. He hadn't been that bad, not bad enough to deserve the terrible punishment of Pirata's loss. Ever since that day on the isola, more than a month ago, he'd been as good as gold and even argued with Tonino that he was wrong about Mama and the teachers and the priests. He'd made vows every day, and kept them. He never wrote his verse, though the professore kept after him, because the only thing to write about was Pirata and he couldn't make pain like that public. But here it was Christmas, and none of the vows had worked—none of the candles, none of the promises, *niente.* Who wouldn't be mad at a Bambino who never listened to kids!

He dodged the cars in the *lungaretta*, swearing, as he'd heard the older boys do. The herb shop was not much farther. He'd get what Mama wanted, go home and let her drag him to church. But he'd close his eyes, and ears, too, and not see or hear anything about Christmas this night.

At a bend in the narrow, twisting street he suddenly stopped, chilled to the bone and very frightened. He felt, he was sure, a hand at the back of his head. But no one stood behind him, the hurrying shoppers indifferent to just another small boy in the crowded street. Still, the invisible hand tightened over his skull and turned his face toward Piazza San Calisto. There, near the portal of the ancient church dedicated to the Virgin, a chestnut vendor huddled forlornly over his brazier. Beside him, heavily chained to the iron axle of a cumbersome wagon, a dog sat erect and expectant. Franco saw the twitch of Pirata's lopsided ear as she waited for his command.

She wasn't much, the vendor assured him, "and if you insist she's yours, you can take her—but only if you buy some chestnuts first. I found this dog half dead, you know, and wanted to give her a good home, but she keeps trying to run away. She'll do the same to you unless you chain her up. Strong as a bull and heavy chain costs money. How much lire do you have, boy; how many chestnuts can you buy?"

Even as one arm held a nuzzling Pirata close, Franco emptied his pocket of all the lire Mama had given him. The vendor smacked his lips in appreciation and filled the largest bag he had with his complete stock of chestnuts. Chestnuts weren't herbs, but the boy knew Mama wouldn't care—though she scolded him to forget Pirata, he'd caught her more than once staring sadly at the dog's cleaned and empty, cupboarded food dish.

Pirata was in good shape—a little lean, and at the moment too excited, but otherwise fine. Franco knelt on the ground in ecstatic communion with her. He'd forgotten the vendor until the man poked him sharply in the ribs, holding aloft the dog's bedraggled collar and leash. "She was dragging this by her mouth when I found her. I planned to sell it but since I haven't more chestnuts to give you for your money, you might as well take it. *Buon Natale, raggazino.*"

The lights of the city were going up as they walked home. And the bells began to ring, the most glorious music Franco had ever heard. Long before he reached his street, he'd quickly composed his verse to

the Bambino. Mama would take him to the Aracoeli—
moaning, no doubt, on each one of the hundred and
twenty-four steps of its steep ascent—but proud to have
him mount the pulpit and recite. He didn't care what
other kids said about little Ciceros. Certainly dogs
weren't admitted inside the Aracoeli. But surely
Professore Bugnini would be there to hear his best
students. Maybe the professore could persuade the
priest to make an exception—just this once—and let
Pirata, too, give thanks to the Bambino.

Don lorenzo

"But Christ was born, and did live, and did die.

No one can take that away from me."

Don lorenzo

I sit with a group of friends for whom the approach of Christmas poses a threat. One of them fears holiday drunkenness and the seasonal binge of her husband. Another speaks of his children's annual disappointment in their gifts, which can't possibly measure up to the glamorous commercial come-ons. An elderly woman who lives alone says it is an especially vicious time of year for those without family or friends. Someone suggests that the holidays are always a time of catharsis, when our anxieties are released in spasms of undisciplined behavior. Suicide statistics soar. A religious man feels that without religion, without faith, Christmas never meets our Great Expectations. We are bitter over the absence of liberating joy which tradition and culture have led us to expect.

From more than one circle of friends, I hear the

groan of despair. How, with political scandals, rampant crime, continuing regional and international wars, punishing economics, environmental crises, and—especially—the collapse of moral and ethical codes, can anyone believe we behave as Christians or that the word and feast have any meaning at all to modern man? Shouldn't we, finally, admit that some primordial need forces us, like the savages and pagans before us, to acknowledge the solstice with Saturnalian bash; and stop kidding ourselves that the holiday in late twentieth century means anything more?

An obstacle to my accepting this argument is the existence of the two children born of our marriage during my middle years. No matter what despairs I bring home from a battered and cynical adult world, they greet me with shining eyes, naiveté, and the simple belief that life is good and Christmas is coming. It is not merely the magic spell of a fairy tale for them. The older child already knows the secret of Santa Claus; knows, too, that the historical Christ entered a world much less romantic than that of the tinseled greeting cards. The doesn't seem to matter. The children know in their hearts, instinctively, that something profound—and good—happens to man at Christmastime.

Don Lorenzo knew it, too. He was a child in no sense, long passed beyond innocence and illusion, harsh as any man I've known. In his late fifties when I met him, father to a young friend of mine, he was a short, thickset man of many moods who frequently brooded and occasionally erupted with fierce outbursts of temper. He had retired from city life and lived at the family's country farm, joined in the summer and over winter holidays by his wife and large clutch of noisy, brilliant, stimulating children.

At first intimidated by his roughness—his angers, profanities and blasphemies—I grew close to him, in time sharing his fondness for wine from his own vineyard, for taking long walks over the fields of Tuscany, and for conversation. At some point during each of my visits to the farm with his fun-loving son, Don Lorenzo and I would desert the elegant country parlor where family and friends dazzled each other with wit, and tramp across the fields, his handsome, faithful setters always nearby. Don Lorenzo was not a reticent man, and I came to know him well.

He mistrusted practically everyone and everything. Governments were universally corrupt—to be despised at all times, and resisted whenever possible. Schools were disastrous, producing charming aristocratic intellectuals like his sons and daughters or blundering civil servants from the middle class, but never educating anyone. The church was a confused bureaucracy managed by spoiled children lining their pockets while lecturing him on the wrong of natural, God-given appetites. People for the most part were no damned good, too sentimental or too brutal, too selfish or piously altruistic, too complaining or long-suffering. He *knew*—he was as bad as the rest, had violated every commandment and wallowed in all the evils.

He had lost or been abandoned by everyone he'd ever loved. Those whom death hadn't claimed in disgusting disease or futile wars, society had wrenched from him through existential philosophy and changing mores. His wife was alienated from him by an identity crisis and sexual confusion which neither of them understood; children were building lives in the new way, divorced from parents; mistresses used him as pragmatically as he used them. Once, as we readied for a summer swim in a swollen river, he removed his clothing in a slow and precise ritual. And perhaps the wine spoke: "Life's like preparing to swim. It strips us of everything."

I remember much, and have forgotten much, that Don Lorenzo said. But this year, with prophets of Humbug proclaiming Christmas a falsehood while my little girls glow with promise and hope, I remember a Midnight Eve when Don Lorenzo was uncharacteristically free of anguish, open and tolerant. I goaded him about the crack in his armor and mercilessly reminded him of the bitter remark on the river bank. "I should have qualified that," he said. "Life strips us of *nearly* everything. But Christ was born, and did live, and did die. No one can take that away from me.

THE NATURE OF GIFTS

"Each letter I opened brought word of new deaths,

deaths of childhood or school friends, neighbors, cousins,

in the Pacific, in the Mediterranean, under the bombs of London

or here on these fields of France."

THE NATURE OF GIFTS

The little children have been very patient in withholding the Magi from their tabletop crèche all through the holidays. But now that Epiphany's here, they lineup Balthazar, Gaspar and Melchior, and express a renewed interest in the Nativity scene—of first priority through Christmas Eve but a bit neglected once the bright packages appeared under the tree.

Our youngest child is curious about those strange-sounding gifts the kings bear. I try to explain the symbolism of their giving, but she is soon distracted. I watch her run after the puppy, who has appropriated her new toy, then I turn to an after-dinner brandy in my hand. I close my eyes, let the aroma permeate my senses, and, relaxing, allow buried images to surface.

We had no brandy snifter, but swilled the cognac from an upturned bottle. And there was precious little of it for three men. Clare and I had conned a young corporal into sharing the last of his gift from an officer, presented to him for performing some humiliating orderly duty. The corporal was soft and homesick, and the brutal holidays had pained him grievously. A sensitive and orthodox boy, he suffered more than most of us, missing the rituals he'd grown up with in rural Pennsylvania, terrified of the horrors on all sides, shocked as much by personal moral collapse as by the immorality of war itself. Even now, as he tried to speak of the feast of Epiphany while Clare and I argued the availability of more cognac, the corporal was staring from a chateau tower-window of our quarters, across snow-blanketed fields, at a tent in the distance. A long line of men, francs in hand, huddled forlornly on the ice, waiting their turns to enter that flimsy, pitiable structure. And inside, the timorous corporal had heard as well as we, was a fourteen-year-old girl from the nearby village.

Clare was holding out. He had some Calvados stashed away somewhere—he always had something— but this day, without denying a hidden reserve, he resolutely refused to produce it. The lines of his face were tauter than ever, his usual rough humor absent.

When I continued to press him about the drink, he unleashed a fury of profanities, saying there were all kinds of untagged wounded, and he was one of them. The liquor was the only medication he could count on, 100-proof guarantee of escape when he needed it. Maybe even a passport to sanity. He was through sharing the booze or anything else with anyone. From this day forward, he would concentrate on survival of Number One. What he had, he'd keep.

I spent the afternoon working alone in Battalion Headquarters, our field cases and other equipment set up haphazardly in the main salon of the once-elegant chateau. Obscene graffiti left behind by Germans who'd used the house before us glared down from paneled walls. Stacks of paperwork, much of it concerning personnel, needed my attention. The outfit had been together three years, and most of the names on reports before me were of men I'd known at one time or another. It was impossible to lose their faces in the statistics of blundering accidents, illness, madness and death. I was convinced that afternoon that the war would never end and that none of us would come out of it alive.

Clare had intercepted a mail-call and brought in a few letters. We stood before a roaring fire on the huge marble hearth and quietly read. Each letter I opened brought word of new deaths, deaths of childhood or school friends, neighbors, cousins, in the Pacific, in the Mediterranean, under the bombs of London or here on these fields of France. And the last was worst of all—a kid sister's fiancé whom I held dear and had hoped to meet on furlough within a month, killed in paratrooper training exercise when his glider disintegrated over Britain. This final, unacceptable blow must have blazoned across my face. For no words passed between us, but Clare stared at me with deep concern. He unhitched the canteen from his cartridge belt, removed its cap, and placed the flask in my hands. It was full to the brim with Calvados, his guarded reserve, his passport to sanity.

Later, when I'd emptied the canteen and wandered aimlessly, staggering blindly over the frozen fields surrounding the chateau, when I had collapsed in a deep drift and surrendered gratefully to oblivion, Clare moved in from the distance at which he had shadowed me. He lugged me back to quarters and silently sat watch by the fire while I slept.

"But what are frankincense and myrrh? And why did the kings bring those?" daughter Daria is asking. Staring into the golden liquid in the brandy glass, pondering the nature of gifts, I do not immediately answer. And then the child is gone again, off on a merry chase through other rooms of the house, and I hear her loud, clear laughter with brothers and sisters.

El santo niño

"Though midnight was hours away,
people were gathered before the church
hopeful of seeing an enactment of the traditional Las Posados."

EL SANTO NIÑO

For the first time since José had carved the
Santo Niño—so many years ago— Lourdes didn't want
to take the figure out of its box to display it for
Christmas. She stared at the wooden torso, the same
size as a real newborn, but felt none of the joy the
annual unwrapping had once given her. She urgently
needed someone to talk to this Christmas Eve; someone
who'd listen. Fear had gripped her all day; she felt
she'd explode if she couldn't share it with another
human being. And this piece of wood, no matter the
pleasure it had afforded in years past, was not human.
It was just something José had made.

And now he was gone, dead almost a year,
victim of a heart attack last January. Just like him, to go
in the fullness of life, without warning, tramping the
snowy foothills one minute, lifeless in a drift the next.

Probably with a smile on his face. He'd be telling her now, if he were still around, to stop worrying, enjoy herself. He'd never been as responsible as she, never took so seriously the demands of home, children, finance. They'd shared little, he with his need of good times, nights out with the boys, hunting and fishing, laughter; she with her seriousness, anchored to the home, contemptuous of frivolity. But they had shared talk, years of it, and he'd never turned away when she had something to tell him, wanted to confide, sought counsel. How many Christmas Eves had he sat at the table listening as she prepared the holiday meal and reported on the children's schoolwork, household accounts, the car, furnace or roofing which needed maintenance, intrigues among the women in her church circles. Now he'd left her; her cares were manifold and there was no one to whom she could tell them.

Certainly not José's wooden *Santo Niño.*

Silence inside the house was broken by the songs of carolers coming from the street. Lourdes impulsively put on her heavy winter coat and tramped out the door into festive *Camino Cañon.* The snow had stopped falling, *luminarias* and *farolitos* burned brightly along the entire length of the narrow road. The crowd of sightseers and revelers was thick. Galleries and shops were open; under their portals, merchants offered hot coffee and toddies to chilled pedestrians, inviting them indoors to the warmth of blazing kiva fireplaces and the seduction of chic wares. All around her, Lourdes heard not only the Spanish and English of Santa Fe, but strange tongues she couldn't fathom. Foreign tourists who in recent years had joined the American visitors daily inundating the road.

Remembering when the street had been primarily residential, when on Christmas Eve it was deserted except for a lone man or boy lighting *farolitos* and stacking wood for *luminarias*, she felt a rush of anger against the commercialism which was turning *Navidad* into carnival. She wondered how many of these strangers knew that the bonfires and candle-lanterns were meant to light the way of *Santo Niño*, to welcome Him into homes.

Homes. Few were left on this glittering thoroughfare of art galleries, restaurants and boutiques. She was one of the last original homeowners still in residence. The neighbors had sold out—or been driven out by property taxes reflecting inflated, gentrified real estate. And how much longer could *she* hold out? What would you have to say to that, José?

Cold, she joined carolers circling a *luminaria* fronting the old Olive Rush house. She recognized no one, but the group was merry and some of the people spoke to her. "Where're you from?" one tourist asked, and when Lourdes replied that she lived on the road, the woman gushed romantic envy about "this enchanting street." Lourdes wanted to tell her about the increased taxes, the very real threat that she'd be forced out of her house, her anguish at no longer being able to afford to live in her ancestral home. But knowing José would frown on that, she spoke about what Christmas Eve here had once been.

"Just a few men, really, tending the fires and *farolitos*. Inviting *El Niño* into their homes. And then, later, small groups of people walking up to Cristo Rey Church, to midnight Mass—old ladies in shawls, fathers towing children on sleds. It was all very still, very holy."

The woman had turned away, was speaking to a man beside her.

Lourdes moved up the street, mindful that most of the carols were secular tunes, not religious hymns. *Jingle Bells*, not *Adeste Fidelis*. But it was hard to fault the revelers for that. She hadn't felt very spiritual herself all this past Advent, not experienced the excitement of anticipating *El Niño*, which had always before been such a joyous part of her holidays.

A portable coffee bar stood before what in the old days had been Gormley's Grocery, was now another art gallery. Lourdes accepted a cup of the steaming brew from the festively-garbed attendant. A young father and his small son had also stopped at the bar and the man was drinking hot cider. Lourdes watched with interest as the boy imitated his father, stamping his feet against the cold whenever the man did. Children were like that. Hers had been, and she wanted to tell the young man about them, tell him to cherish that youngster now, while he had him, because they all eventually move away—say they can't afford Santa Fe—and communication grows infrequent, grandchildren are born whom one rarely sees. But José nudged her, so she said none of that, merely smiled at the father and commented "What a beautiful child." The young man apparently didn't hear her, was waving a greeting to friends across the road and, gathering the boy in his arms, took off in their direction.

She was sure José would have enjoyed the spectacle: bonfires in the street, *farolitos* lining curbs and footpaths, strung along rooftops and on adobe walls; milling crowds; festive song; free refreshments; bright shops with dazzling displays. But Lourdes drifted east, where shops were fewer and the crowd thinned. From long habit, she climbed the hill toward Cristo Rey, where she'd been married, where her children had been baptized. Though midnight was hours away, people were gathered before the church hopeful of seeing an enactment of the traditional *Las Posados*. Strangers again, some obviously tourists clutching programs of Santa Fe's scheduled Christmas events.

And then, among the sea of *forasteros*, she glimpsed a former neighbor, Consuelo, one of the last to sell her home on the road and move away. Lourdes almost fell into her arms. Here was someone she'd always been able to talk to.

"Feliz Navidad," Consuelo greeted her. "I had to come back to my old church tonight. Nowhere else like Cristo Rey on Christmas Eve." She spoke about her new neighborhood, friends she'd made there. And she asked if Lourdes would be attending Midnight Mass.

"It's difficult for me," Lourdes said. "Like a crisis of faith, you know. Not just José dying and the kids being far away. Everything, our whole society. Everything obscene and violent. The newspapers, the TV, being disenfranchised in one's own home town, feeling betrayed on all sides. The sex scandals among clergy in our archdiocese."

Consuelo drew back in alarm. "The media exaggerates everything, Lourdes. You mustn't believe all you read or hear."

"One can't deny reality. We no longer live like Christians, Consuelo, we're a pagan culture." This was what she'd really wanted to talk about all day, to José, to anyone who'd listen—about her hurt, her pain at the loss of belief and values which had sustained her throughout life. But Consuelo was backing away and quickly fled, escaping into families gathered before the church door. From inside the church came the strains of the traditional hymn *Vamos a Belen*, soft, beautiful, moving. Lourdes turned away from the music and started home.

The phone was ringing when she entered her house. Linda, calling from California. "Mom, I can't talk long but just had to know if you're all right. We're in the middle of a party, friends here, the kids into everything, but I said to Eddie 'It's Christmas Eve, and I've got to call my Mom.' Had to know you're all right."

All right? I miss your Dad, I miss you, my arms ache to hold my grandchildren, Lourdes thought. I live among strangers in a city I no longer know, can't pay the taxes and may lose my home. I'm lost in an alien world, offended by its vileness, terrified by its violence. I can't approach my church.

"Linda, it's so good to hear your voice. There's so much I want to tell you."

"I can't talk now, Mom. But I'll call again. After the new year. Just wanted to know you're all right. You *are* all right, Mom?"

"Go back to your friends, Linda. *Feliz Navidad.*"

It was very quiet after she'd hung up the phone. Not even the carolers could be heard in the street. She stood again over José's carved *Santo Niño*, looking at its mute mouth, touching the folds of swaddling which José's hands had sculpted. It really was a good carving, not of just any *niño*, but of *El Santo Niño*, reverent, imbued with that tenderness which had occasionally surfaced—and surprised her—in her rough husband. She remembered José saying on so many Christmas Eves that *El Niño* never failed you. Everything else could fail—your spouse, your children, the government, the church, and you could fail yourself, but *El Niño* would always be there.

Lourdes rested her head on the table beside the carving, wept a little and told Him everything.

"Today in the town of David a savior has been born to you;

he is Christ the Lord."

The Gospel According to Saint Luke

GLOSSARY

Spanish:

abuelo - grandfather

adobe - sun-dried brick, adobe house

Buen Señor - Good Lord

burro - donkey

Camino Cañon - Canyon Road

comida - food, meal

campesinos - country men, peasants

El Buen Pastor - The Good Shepherd

farolitos - lanterns; in New Mexico, vigil candles in
    sand-filled paper bags

Feliz Navidad - Merry Christmas

frijoles - beans

gracias - thanks

Jesuscristo - Jesus Christ

Jesus Es Mi Amor - traditional hymn, Jesus is my love

las Posados - the Inns; traditional New Mexico
    Christmas pageant "no room at the inn."

la tierra - the land, earth

luminarias - in New Mexico, bonfires lighted on
    Christmas Eve

mi hija - my child

muchacho - boy

nacimiento - birth; in New Mexico, the Christmas
    creche

Nuestra Señora - Our Lady

niña - girl

noche de paz - night of peace

norteamericano - North American

pastores - shepherds

piñon - pine nut, also refers to specific pine tree in New
    Mexico

poncho - a blanket-like cloak

rebozo - scarf or shawl

San José - Saint Joseph

santero - saint-maker; artisan of religious figures

santuario - shrine

Santo Niño - Holy Child

señor - mister, Mr, Sir

taco - tortilla wrapped around meat or cheese

tierra encantada - enchanted land

Vamos Todas a Belen - Come to Bethlehem, traditional
    hymn

vigas - beams, rafters

Italian:

Buon Natale - Merry Christmas

calcio - soccer

Campo dei Fiori - Field of Flowers

Gesu - Jesus

Il Messaggero - messenger; in Rome, name of a
    newspaper

Isola Tiberina - little island in the Tiber River

lungaretta - long street in Trastevere district, Rome

Piazza Bocca della Verita - Square of the Mouth of
    Truth

Piazza di Spagna - Spanish Square

Piazza San Calisto - St Calisto's Square

presepio - creche

raggazino - young boy

Santa Maria Aracoeli - St Mary of Heaven's Altar

Santo Bambino - Holy Infant

signori - gentlemen

Stazione Termini - Rome's main railroad station

www.ingramcontent.com/pod-product-compliance
Lightning Source LLC
Chambersburg PA
CBHW010834250626
47157CB00010B/3283